Treasure in the Attic

Story by Alan Trussell-Cullen

Illustrations by Elise Hurst

Contents

Chapter 1

The Best Teacher

"Here we are at last,"
said Abby's and Zoe's mother.
They stopped outside a big, old house.
It was at the top of a hill
looking out over Pirates Bay.

"It's like a house from a story book," said Abby.

"Or a movie," said Zoe.

"And we're right on time," said Mum.
"We can't be late for Mrs Patterson."

"But who is she?" asked Zoe.

"I was in her class at school," said Mum. "She was the best teacher I ever had."

Mrs Patterson gave Mum a great big hug. "And you must be Abby and Zoe!" she said. "What is it like to be twins?"

"Most of the time it's fun," said Abby. "But it's annoying if people mistake me for Zoe."

"Or when they mistake me for Abby," said Zoe.

"Do you ever get muddled yourselves?" asked Mrs Patterson.

The twins laughed. "Oh, no!" they said.

"Even when we look at photos of us as babies, we can tell if it's Zoe or me," said Abby.

Mrs Patterson looked hard at the twins.

"Can you tell who we are?" asked Abby.

"I think so," said Mrs Patterson.
"You're Abby. And you're Zoe."

"Yes!" laughed the girls.

"Mrs Patterson never forgets a face!" said Mum.

Chapter 2

The Star Pupil

Mum, Abby and Zoe followed Mrs Patterson
into the living room
where Mrs Patterson had a cup of tea waiting.

Mum and Mrs Patterson talked
about Mum's school days,
while Abby and Zoe sat and listened.

8

"Did Mum get into a lot of trouble
at school?" asked Zoe.

Mrs Patterson laughed. "No," she said.
"Your mother was my star pupil!
But this must be boring for you.
What do you think of my house?"

"It's very old," said Abby.
"Does it have any secret passageways?"

"That's Pirates Bay down there, isn't it?"
said Zoe.
"Maybe pirates lived here in the old days
and hid their gold underneath the floorboards."

Mrs Patterson laughed and said,
"I don't know about any secret passageways
or pirates' gold.
But we might find some treasure upstairs
in the attic."

"Real treasure?" said Abby.

"Like jewels and bars of gold?" said Zoe.

"I'm not sure," said Mrs Patterson.

Chapter 3

In the Attic

Mrs Patterson gave Mum a secret smile
and said to the girls,
"Let's go up to the attic
and have a look for treasure, shall we?"

The twins raced up the stairs.

But when Mrs Patterson opened the attic door, the twins were disappointed.
All they could see were old chairs and boxes.

"This doesn't look like treasure, Mrs Patterson," said Abby.

Chapter 4

Finding Treasure

"Oh, there's treasure here all right,"
said Mrs Patterson. "I'll find some for you!"

She began to hunt through a pile of papers.
"Here we are!" she said.

"But that's an old school photo,
Mrs Patterson," said Abby.
"What's special about it?"

"Look at the back row," said Mrs Patterson.

"That's Zoe!" said Abby.
"What's she doing in this old photo?"

"No, it's not!" said Zoe. "That's you, Abby!"

Mum and Mrs Patterson began to laugh.

"You're both wrong," said Mrs Patterson. "It's someone who looked like both of you when she was your age."

"I know who it is!" gasped Abby.

"Me, too!" said Zoe.

"It's Mum!" they both shouted.

"Yes," said Mrs Patterson.
"I told you there was treasure in here!
You can take it home with you, if you like.
It could be the start of your very own treasure."

The twins smiled. "Thank you, Mrs Patterson!"
they said together.